DATE DUE

THE NOISES ANIMALS MAKE

ISBN 0-89868-312-2—Library Bound
ISBN 0-89868-313-0—Soft Bound

A PREDICTABLE WORD BOOK

THE NOISES ANIMALS MAKE

Story by Janie Spaht Gill, Ph.D.
Illustrations by Lori Anderson Wing

ARO PUBLISHING

A wolf says to a wolf,
"Let's howl."

4

A bear says to a bear,
"Let's growl."

An owl says
to an owl,

"Let's hoo."

A cow says to a cow,

"Let's moo."

11

A bird says to a bird,
"Let's tweet."

A mouse says to a mouse,

"Let's squeak."

A goose says to a goose,
"Let's honk."

A dog says to a dog,

"Let's bark."

A chicken says to a chicken,

"Let's squawk."

But I say
to a friend,
"Let's talk."